Living as LGBTQ+

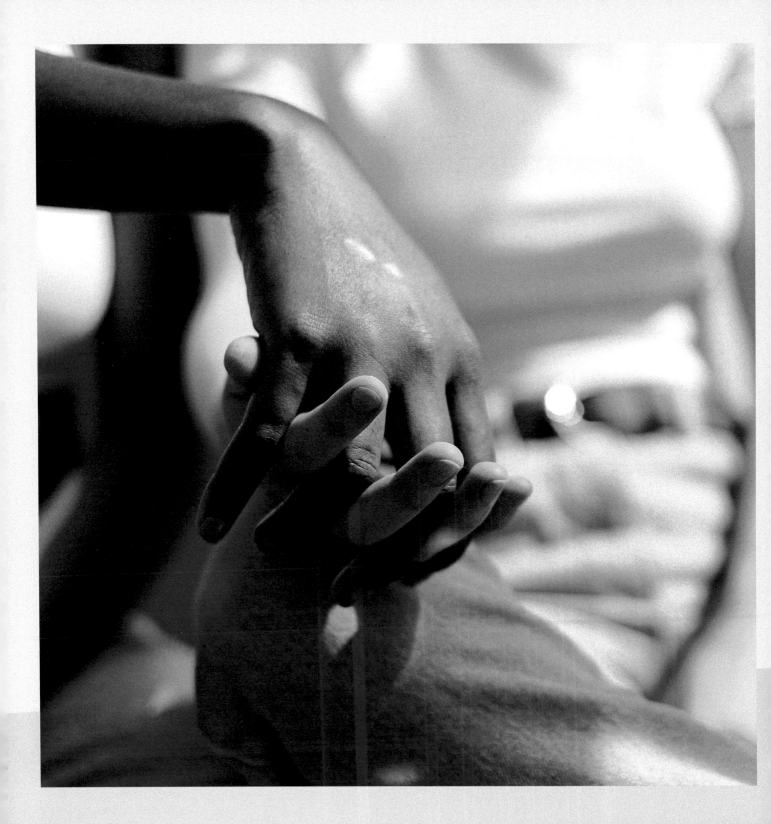

Living as LGBTQ+

D. S. Strode

Living in AMERICA

CREATIVE EDUCATION

CREATIVE PAPERBACKS

Published by Creative Education and Creative Paperbacks
P.O. Box 227, Mankato, Minnesota 56002
Creative Education and Creative Paperbacks are imprints
of The Creative Company
www.thecreativecompany.us

Book design by Graham Morgan (www.bluedes.com)
Art direction by Tom Morgan
Edited by Jill Kalz

Images by Getty Images/Bettmann, 13, Catherine McGann, 18,
Maskot, 28, 36, Mark Mulligan, 31, New York Daily News Archive,
17, Rossella De Berti, 42–43, SolStock, 6–7, Stephen Maturen, 35;
National Archives, 27; Pexels/Anna Shvets, 2; Shutterstock/Marc
Bruxelle, 4–5, Rena Schild, 32; Unsplash/Alexander Grey, 22, Diogo
Fagundes, 1, Leighann Blackwood, 8–9, Margaux Bellott, 20–21,
Raphael Renter | @raphi_rawr, 38–39; Wellcome Collection, 15;
Wikimedia Commons, 10–11, Allan Warren, 44, Gillman & Co, 24,
NIAID, 14, Pax Ahimsa Gethen, 45 Raimond Spekking / CC BY-SA
4.0, 40, Shirley Smith, 31

Library of Congress Cataloging-in-Publication Data
Names: Strode, D. S., author.
Title: Living as LGBTQ+ / by D. S. Strode.
Description: Mankato, Minnesota : Creative Education and Creative
    Paperbacks, [2025] | Series: Living in america | Includes
    bibliographical references and index. | Audience: Ages 12–15 |
    Audience: Grades 7–9 | Summary: "A social studies title for young
    adults that examines the history of the lesbian, gay, bisexual,
    transgender, queer, and more (LGBTQ+) community in the United
    States of America. Includes sidebars, real-person profiles, a
    glossary, a timeline, and further resources"—Provided by
    publisher.
Identifiers: LCCN 2023046955 (print) | LCCN 2023046956 (ebook)
    | ISBN 9781640269095 (library binding) | ISBN 9781682774595
    (paperback) | ISBN 9798889890775 (ebook)
Subjects: LCSH: Sexual minorities—United States—Juvenile
    literature. | Sexual minorities—Legal status, laws, etc.—United
    States. | Human rights—United States—Juvenile literature. | Gay
    rights—United States—Juvenile literature.
Classification: LCC HQ73.3.U6 S44 2025 (print) | LCC HQ73.3.U6
    (ebook) | DDC 306.760973—dc23/eng/20231120
LC record available at https://lccn.loc.gov/2023046955
LC ebook record available at https://lccn.loc.gov/2023046956

Printed in China

CONTENTS

Introduction 8

Chapter 1: Making History 11

    ZOOM IN: FACTS ABOUT AIDS 14

    ZOOM IN: REAGAN'S SILENCE 16

Chapter 2: Standing Proud 20

    ZOOM IN: WHAT'S IN A NAME? 23

    ZOOM IN: THE 14TH AMENDMENT 26

Chapter 3: Struggles and Challenges 29

    ZOOM IN: REASONS FOR BANNING 30

    ZOOM IN: SAFE STATES 34

Chapter 4: Ever Forward 38

    ZOOM IN: FINDING REFUGE 40

    ZOOM IN: QUEER JOY 42

Getting Real: 44

    JAMES BALDWIN 44

    ZOOEY ZEPHYR 45

Timeline 46

Glossary 47

Selected Bibliography 47

Websites 47

Index 48

Introduction

Lesbian, gay, bisexual, transgender, queer, and more. This is what the letters *LGBTQ+* stand for. They represent a community full of vibrant people who live all around the world. Women who are attracted to other women identify as lesbian, while men attracted to other men identify as gay. Bisexual individuals are attracted to both women and men. People who do not identify as their assigned gender at birth are considered transgender. Queer is a term for anyone who isn't cisgender or straight. And the plus sign stands for identities not on this list. In the United States, the LGBTQ+ community makes up just over 7 percent of the population.

The nation's relationship with the LGBTQ+ community throughout history has been complicated. There have been wins and losses, celebrations and dark days. The country has shown its citizens great love and great hate. Largely because of the struggles and challenges they've faced, members of the LGBTQ+ community today have renewed strength and conviction. Now more than ever, queer people are showing the world who they are—on television, on the radio, in the books they write, and across the Internet. And queer youth are seeing themselves represented in record numbers.

America's LGBTQ+ community has come a long way toward acceptance and equality. But there is still a long way to go.

San Francisco's city hall is lit up in rainbow colors for Pride.

Centuries ago, sodomy laws meant that gay people could face the death penalty if caught.

CHAPTER 1

Making History

Laws against queer people have existed in the United States for centuries—even before the country was officially a country! When a religious group called the Puritans left England in the 1600s, they settled in **colonies** along what is now the U.S. East Coast.

Puritans had a strict way of thinking, and it influenced the laws they made. In their view, sex was only for making children. This meant same-sex relationships were forbidden. At first, the penalty for breaking these laws (called sodomy laws) was death. In 1682, that changed. Offenders would no longer face the death penalty. Instead, they risked whipping, having land taken from them, being forced into hard labor, or going to jail.

Colonial America was a long time ago, but that strict view continues to impact queer people today. Many religious and political groups across the country think that same-sex attractions are "unnatural." They believe being transgender is "sinful" or a result of mental illness. They fail to see queer people for who they are at their core—fellow human beings.

In the 1860s, a transgender man named Albert Cashier joined the army to fight in the Civil War (1861–65). He had been dressing as a boy from a young age to find jobs and support his family. When he enlisted, no one questioned his need for privacy while bathing and getting dressed. When his time with the army ended, he moved back to his home state of Illinois.

One day, Cashier was hit by a car and sent to the town doctor for treatment. His secret was revealed, and life as he knew it was at stake. He risked losing his status as a war veteran and his veteran pay. If found out, he would be forced to live as a woman, the gender he was assigned at birth. Luckily, the doctor and the nurses who took care of him agreed to keep his secret.

Not everyone was so kind. In 1914, after life had worn down his body and mind, Cashier was sent to Waterstone State Hospital for the Insane. Once again, his secret was exposed. This time, the newspapers brought it to the public's attention. Cashier was charged with tricking, or defrauding, the government to get veteran pay. But his fellow soldiers stuck up for him. They told stories about his many brave actions during the war. In the end, Cashier was allowed to keep his veteran status and pay, but he was forced to wear women's clothes for the rest of his life. He died one year later, in 1915, and received the full military burial he deserved.

During World War I (1914–18) and World War II (1939–45), most women in the United States stayed on the home front and did the jobs that were typically done by men. This led to

Women in same-sex relationships, such as Carrie Chapman Catt (center) and Mary Garrett (right), often faced unjust treatment.

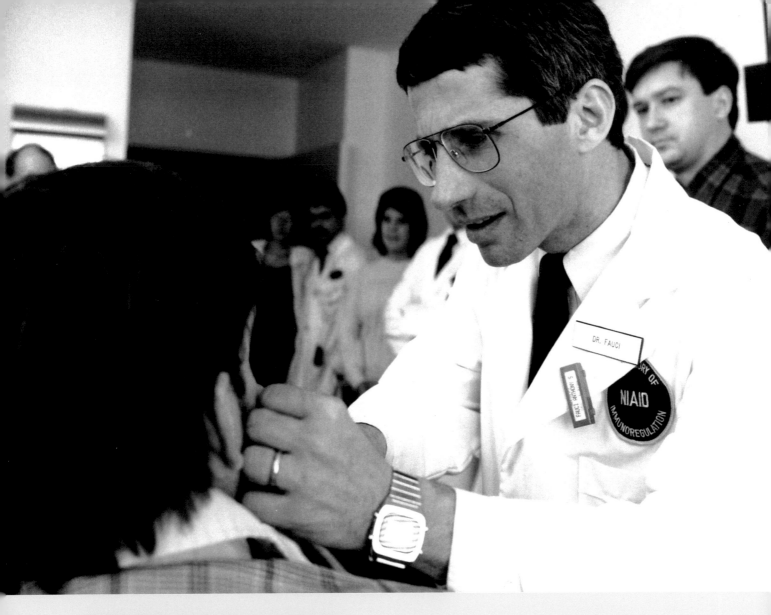

ZOOM IN: FACTS ABOUT AIDS

- AIDS can be spread through bodily fluids exchanged during sex, shared syringes, and breast feeding. It cannot be transmitted through saliva, touching, sweat, or sharing food.
- HIV stands for human immunodeficiency virus. It weakens a person's immune system by destroying important cells that fight disease and infection. AIDS is the most advanced form of HIV.
- Gay people are not the only ones who can get HIV/AIDS.
- At the peak of the AIDS epidemic (1987–98), more than 324,000 people died of the disease.

the organization of the Women's Rights Movement. Women wanted the same rights as men and to be able to work even when the men *weren't* off at war. This movement would have a huge impact on the lesbian community. At the time, women were not able to vote or work jobs to support themselves. They needed to marry a man or rely on other men in their families. But if women were allowed to support themselves, then lesbian partners would be able to thrive on their own. So, that is exactly what they fought for.

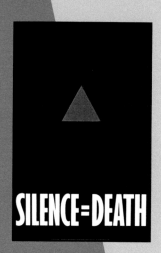

SILENCE=DEATH

The pink triangle is a pro-gay symbol.
Activists created the Silence = Death
campaign in 1987 to increase awareness
of the AIDS epidemic.

Many of the women's voting rights leaders of the National American Woman Suffrage Association (NAWSA) were described as having lesbian-like lifestyles. Jane Addams and her partner, Mary Rozet Smith, were known to support each other financially and emotionally. They would often write loving letters to each other. Carrie Chapman Catt and Mary Garrett Hay lived together after the death of Catt's second husband. When Catt died, she chose to be buried next to Hay instead of either of her husbands. The women's headstone reads: "Here lie two, united in friendship for thirty-eight years through constant service to a great cause." Sophonisba Breckinridge, too, was known to have an intimate relationship with Marion Talbot and later Edith Abbott. None of these women were publicly "out." However, their letters and life partners lead historians to believe they might have been more than "just friends," as history originally painted them to be.

Before the 1960s, most queer people hid who they were from the public eye. There were a lot of consequences to worry about, and most people just wanted to be safe. There were laws in place that forbid same-sex couples from going to bars and restaurants. Dancing together was against the law. When the LGBTQ+ community set up their own spaces to meet and hang out, police came and shut them down, sometimes arresting individuals.

Pressures were rising in the United States, and a time of change was on the horizon. Organizations formed to provide community support and legal aid to queer people who wanted to fight back against discrimination and homophobia. Craig Roswall was a man with a passion for reform and change. He came up with the idea to picket at government buildings every year to remind lawmakers that queer people still did not have equal rights in America. The event became known as the Annual Reminders. It started in 1965 with 35 attendees. There was a strict dress code to ensure people saw LGBTQ+ community members as proper, upright citizens.

The Annual Reminders ended in 1969, shortly after the Stonewall Riots in New York City. That violent clash between law enforcement and the gay community changed the energy in the air. The time for

ZOOM IN: REAGAN'S SILENCE

In times of crisis, people turn to their leaders for guidance. During the early years of the AIDS epidemic, however, U.S. president Ronald Reagan and his administration remained silent about the matter. For five years, the only mentions of AIDS in press interviews were jokes and dismissive comments. When famous actor (and family friend) Rock Hudson died of AIDS in 1985, Reagan finally spoke up. He funded research to determine what caused AIDS and declared it a public health priority. While his change in policies helped put an end to the epidemic, his five years of silence would have a long-lasting impact on the country.

Gay and lesbian people refused to leave when police raided the Stonewall Inn on June 28, 1969, setting off riots that lasted for days.

peaceful picketing had passed. Queer people were done hiding and pretending to be "normal" to fit in. That fateful day in June, a spark was lit in the hearts of queer people across the country.

Despite its impact on history, the Stonewall Riots didn't fix all the problems the LGBTQ+ community faced. Queer people were still seen as the enemy and as outsiders. From 1945 to 1991, the United States was engaged in the Cold War with the former Soviet Union. It was a time of intense hostility between the two superpowers. People in the United States were full of fear. This fear was behind the Lavender Scare, which started in the 1950s and continued for decades. During this time in history, it was dangerous to be different. If you were suspected of being a Communist spy for the Soviet Union, you could be fired from your job or arrested. Because queer people already existed outside society's standards, they were suspected of being easy

targets for Communist blackmail. Employees were fired from their government jobs and shunned by their neighbors.

The gay community was shunned again in the 1980s. A disease called Acquired Immune Deficiency Syndrome (AIDS) swept across the country. Early on, people didn't know much about AIDS or how it spread. One common misconception was that only gay men could get it. While gay men were the ones most infected with the disease, everyone was at risk.

At the beginning of the AIDS crisis, the U.S. government failed to take seriously the reports of healthy men suddenly getting sick and dying. Some people thought the men had a rare form of cancer. One gay man named Larry Kramer sensed that something wasn't right, and in 1981, he collected donations to fund research of the mysterious disease. If no one else was going to help the queer community, then it would have to help itself. And it did. Across the United States, organizations such as the Gay Men's Health Crisis (GMHC) and ACT UP were formed to help with mutual aid. Food was distributed. Research was conducted. Volunteers stayed at the bedsides of dying patients who had often been abandoned by their families.

In 1987, a drug called azidothymidine (AZT) was developed. It slowed the symptoms of AIDS and helped patients live longer. But it was not a cure. Developments in medicine have continued over the years; however, there is still no cure for the disease. People around the world still struggle with the effects of AIDS to this day.

If no one else was going to help the queer community, then it would have to help itself.

Larry Kramer was an outspoken AIDS activist as well as an author and playwright.

People cheer and wave rainbow flags in support of the LGBTQ+ community at a Pride parade.

CHAPTER 2:

Standing Proud

t's a hot, sunny weekend in June. The air is buzzing with excitement as people line the streets. There are teens with flags tied like capes around their shoulders, people dancing, and the distant sounds of music as a parade rounds the bend.

The LGBTQ+ community is gathered for its yearly Pride parade. Held in cities across the country, Pride parades bring people together to watch performances, share food and drink, and celebrate their freedom to love whomever they choose.

The first Pride parades in the United States happened in 1970. Before that time, queer people largely lived in the shadows. Businesses could deny service to them, and it was illegal for same-sex couples to be together in public. Because of this, queer people established bars of their own, where they would be safe to meet and hang out with others in their communities. One such bar was the Stonewall Inn in New York City. In the late 1960s, it was known as a place where queer people could come and express themselves. The police were aware of this, too, and they often came to break up the party and harass the patrons of the bar. On the night of June 28, 1969, the police did just that.

Tensions had been building in the community, and the night of June 28 served as the spark that lit a revolution for LGBTQ+ people. A lesbian woman known as Storme DeLarverie was arrested by police at the Stonewall Inn. As they took her away, she called out to others in the bar for help. There are many different accounts of what happened that night, but some say that DeLarverie threw the first punch that spurred everyone else into action.

For six days, queer people fought against police brutality. They marched in the streets and made their voices heard. They were tired of being mistreated by the government and their neighbors. They made banners and wore armbands that showed they were proud of being queer.

On the one-year anniversary of the Stonewall Riots, in 1970, thousands of people gathered in New York; Chicago, Illinois; and Los Angeles, California, to march in the first Pride parades. They wanted to show the world that they were unashamed and joyful about their identities as lesbian and gay (bisexual and trans were later added to the LGBTQ+ acronym). Over the years, the number of Pride parades has grown. They are held in cities big and small. In 1999, President Bill Clinton declared June to be Lesbian and Gay Pride Month. In 2011, President Barack Obama changed it to include the entire LGBTQ+ community.

Pride has changed a lot since the first parades. People show up dressed in their Pride flag clothes and glittery makeup. In some locations, once the parade goes by, everyone watching from the sidelines joins at the end. Together, they march down the street in a river of bright colors and laughter. It is a time of reflection and thankfulness for all the people whose work and sacrifice brought the LGBTQ+ community to where it is today. It is a time to support one another in the ongoing battles to gain equality. It is a time to tell the nation and the world, "I am queer, and I deserve to exist."

In times before parades, when being queer was often dangerous and needed to be hidden, people invented ways to indicate to each other that they were also queer. People still use some of these symbols, mainly to honor the community's past. New symbols have also been adopted. They represent different genders and sexualities. Lavender, ace rings, pride flags, and a stuffed blue shark all have special meaning.

Lavender The color lavender, as well as the flower for which it is named, is a symbol of empowerment and resistance. In the late 1800s, wearing this color was a way for people to cast off social norms and express themselves. Popular poet Oscar Wilde often wore a lavender waistcoat with a green carnation to show that he was queer. So did his friends and followers. Later, in 1969, protesters at the Stonewall Riots wore lavender armbands and sashes.

Ace Ring In 2005, members of the asexual community created their own symbol. They started wearing a black ring on the middle finger of their right hand. It indicated that they were a part of the asexual, or Ace, community. Asexuals are people who have little to no interest in having sex with anyone.

Pride Flags In 1978, Gilbert Baker designed the iconic flag that defines the Pride movement. His first version was a little different than today's. It featured a hot pink stripe above the red and two shades of blue. Hot pink cloth was hard for people to find, so the flag was revised. The following year, the pink was dropped, and the turquoise stripe was omitted, leaving an even number of stripes. Two new flags debuted in 2017 and 2018 respectively. The Philadelphia Pride flag included a black stripe and a brown stripe to recognize people of color in the community. The Progress flag added a V-shaped mark, or chevron, to the classic Pride flag. The chevron was made up of pink, white,

Oscar Wilde (1854–1900, *left*), an Irish writer, wore a flower as a signal to others that he was gay. He was later imprisoned for homosexuality.

and blue stripes for the trans community, brown for people of color, and black to pay tribute to the lives lost to AIDS.

Blåhaj the Shark In 2020, an Internet meme was made about the Blåhaj (bloh-HI) shark from the home goods store Ikea. The shark has been around since 2014. Its name simply means "blue shark." Young adults on the TikTok app and Reddit website made posts declaring Blåhaj to be an ally to the LGBTQ+ community. Some say it is because the shark has the same colors as the transgender flag. Whatever the reason, it has quickly become a way for trans people to bond over the Internet.

While the LGBTQ+ community embraced these symbols as their own, they were thrilled to share another with the straight community in 2015: wedding rings. On June 26, 2015, the U.S. Supreme Court made the decision to legalize same-sex marriage. It was a historic day in the nation's history. However, the road to marriage equality hadn't been an easy one.

In the 1990s, people began challenging the laws at both state and federal levels. They requested that same-sex couples receive the same rights as straight couples. In most places, the laws surrounding marriage were based on men marrying women. In 1996, the Defense of Marriage Act (DOMA) was passed. This law made it official that marriage was defined at the federal level as a union between a man and a woman.

ZOOM IN: THE 14TH AMENDMENT

The 14th Amendment to the U.S. Constitution played a key role in achieving marriage equality in the LGBTQ+ community. It states, "No State shall . . . deny to any person within its jurisdiction the equal protection of the laws." It was approved, or ratified, in 1868 to establish legal and civil rights for formerly enslaved people. Since then, it has continued to ensure equal rights for all U.S. citizens, including women, people of color, immigrants, and the LGBTQ+ community.

The 14th Amendment to the U.S. Constitution promises equal rights to all citizens.

Seventeen years later, DOMA was declared unconstitutional. This was a huge step toward equality. In 2015, a case called *Oberfell v. Hodges* was voted on in the Supreme Court. Many queer couples gathered in Washington, D.C., and waited anxiously. The case asked two very important questions: (1) Does the 14th Amendment require a state to license a marriage between two people of the same sex? (2) Does the 14th Amendment require a state to recognize a marriage between two people of the same sex that was legally licensed and performed in another state?

The nine Supreme Court justices voted, and their answer was yes. No matter what U.S. state the couple was in, they could be married. And the union would have to be recognized in the same way as a marriage between a man and woman.

CHAPTER 3:

Struggles and Challenges

Living as a queer person in the United States can be challenging. The ideals that were held to be true for the Puritans in the 1600s still carry weight today. Many queer Americans face discrimination at work or school, from their families, and in public spaces.

It often seems that when the community clears one obstacle, more arise to replace it. Lawmakers have banned books containing LGBTQ+ characters, made laws that force trans children away from their families, and denied access to important health care.

Books are banned in school and public libraries for many reasons. Those with LGBTQ+ themes might go against a family's religious or political views. Books with sexual content, swearing, or violence can be seen as inappropriate for younger age groups who might not be ready for that kind of material. All parents want to protect their children from things that may negatively impact

Same-sex couples may feel safe at home but face discrimination out in the world.

them. But some parents want to do so by eliminating access to the books altogether.

On the other side of the issue are the educators, librarians, and parents who want people to have access to books that represent many diverse communities, including LGBTQ+. They believe it is the parent or guardian's right and responsibility to judge what is right for their own children, but not for everyone. Seeing diverse communities in books and media can be affirming for the people in those communities. It can also help others learn more about the world around them.

Since 2003, when the American Library Association (ALA) started collecting data, the number of challenged books has trended upward each year. The year 2022 set a record. A total of 2,571 books received demands to censor. Most of them were about or written by people of color and the LGBTQ+ community. In 2022, the most challenged book was *Gender Queer* by nonbinary and asexual author Maia Kobabe. It was targeted due to "sexually explicit and LGBTQ+ content." Other books, such as *To Kill a Mockingbird* by Harper Lee, are frequently challenged because of the "explicit language and racial slurs." Every year, the ALA hosts Banned Books Week. During the event, libraries across the country make displays and host programs that educate their communities about banned books and how banning can be harmful.

ZOOM IN: REASONS FOR BANNING

Books are often challenged by people who want to protect children from difficult ideas and information. To an extent, this is a noble mission. But it can quickly become a problem when entire communities are deemed "inappropriate." It is important for kids to see themselves reflected in the books they read. This includes not only queer kids but kids of all races, abilities, interests, and backgrounds. These are the top 10 reasons cited for banning books:

1. LGBTQ+ Content
2. Sexually Explicit
3. Profanity
4. Racism
5. Violence
6. Religious Viewpoints
7. Sex Education
8. Suicide
9. Drug and Alcohol Use
10. Nudity

JEWELL PARKER RHODES   GHOS

THE GLASS CASTLE   JEANNETTE

EVISON   LAWN BOY

RAINA TELGEMEIER

THIS BOOK IS GAY   JU
DAWS

THOMAS   THE HATE U GIV

JOHNSON   ALL BOYS AREN'T BLUE

GENDER QUEER   MAIA KOBABE

In states such as Florida and Texas, book challenges are at an all-time high. But that is not the only growing problem facing queer families, especially in the southern states. In May 2023, Florida governor Ron DeSantis passed bills that caused many queer families with children to leave the state. In their eyes, the bills were designed to force the LGBTQ+ community back into the shadows.

One of Florida's bills is the Don't Say LGBTQ+ Expansion Bill. It makes it illegal for teachers to talk about sexual orientation or gender identity in their classrooms. It also requires them to deadname and misgender students.

The Extreme Gender Affirming Care Ban, officially known as SB254, prohibits doctors and medical professionals from giving gender affirming care to their patients. If they do, they can be charged with a felony and have their medical license canceled. If the State of Florida deems a child "at risk" of receiving gender affirming care, that child can be removed from their family.

Florida's HB1521 law bans transgender people from using the bathroom that matches their gender identity. So, for example, if someone was assigned female at birth, they must use the women's bathroom. The bill also bans gender-inclusive bathrooms in schools, jails, and health care spaces. Similar bills are proposed and voted on nearly every day.

While some states pass laws that harm the LGBTQ+ community, others work to provide a safe place for families to find shelter.

Minnesota's governor, Tim Walz, passed an executive order in March 2023 that made the state a "trans refuge state." This order protects trans people, their families, and their medical providers. Minnesota isn't the only state doing this. Colorado, New Mexico, Illinois, and Maryland have also passed protective laws to support the trans community.

Many anti-trans laws revolve around health care. "Gender affirming care" is a term used in the trans community to describe resources used to change oneself, or transition. There are three main types of transitioning: physical, social, and legal. Physical transitioning is when a person alters their appearance to fit their gender identity. This could include wearing a binder to flatten the chest, cutting one's hair, taking hormones, or having surgeries. Social transitioning is when a person changes their name, pronouns, or clothing. "Coming out" is part of social transitioning. It is the time when a person tells their friends and family that they are a member of the LGBTQ+ community. Legal transitioning is when a person's name or the gender marker on their government ID is changed.

While most trans people transition in one way or another, it is not the same for everyone. Each person is on their own path.

In 2023, there was a rise in states passing bills that were dangerous for families with transgender children. Some of these families moved to safer states to prevent forced detransitioning and separation. Several factors are used to determine if a state is considered safe. They include nondiscrimination laws, hate crime laws, access to transgender health care, LGBTQ+ population density, and conversion therapy laws. Considering all of these factors, the following five states are considered the friendliest for LGBTQ+ people:

- District of Columbia
- Massachusetts
- California
- Vermont
- New York

Governor Tim Walz of Minnesota has made his state welcoming to trans people.

Sometimes, all it takes to feel comfortable in one's body is a haircut and a change of pronouns. Other people may need a gender affirming surgery to feel whole. Transitioning often takes a long time, and the path may change along the way. That's why it's important for trans people have access to qualified therapists or counselors who can give guidance.

When people don't have the support they need and are not able to transition, it can cause serious harm. Gender dysphoria is when the sex a person was assigned at birth does not match the gender they identify with. In addition to causing discomfort, it can cause trans people to become depressed or anxious about their bodies. Living with gender dysphoria for a long time, with no gender affirming care, has led many people to commit suicide. In 2022, more than 40 percent of trans youth in the United States seriously considered taking their own lives. The percentage is higher for trans youth who are also Indigenous or people of color.

It's important for trans people have access to qualified therapists or counselors who can give guidance.

The *opposite* is true for queer youth who have supportive homes or schools. They feel happier, safer, and less alone. Examples of support include schools using preferred names and having LGBTQ+ clubs. At home, having parents who listen and are willing to help their child thrive is a great support. The simple act of accepting someone regardless of gender or sexuality could save a life.

CHAPTER 4:

Ever Forward

America's LGBTQ+ community **advocates** for its members in many ways. The Human Rights Campaign is a well-known civil rights group that was formed in 1980 by a gay man named Steve Endean.

Over the past 40+ years, the group has worked hard to achieve equal rights for the LGBTQ+ community. It provides education and outreach programs for parents, educators, and allies. Its website includes the history of the LGBTQ+ community, proper pronoun usage, and current LGBTQ+ events.

In 2021, a new organization was founded called Queer Youth Assemble. What makes it unique is that it is entirely run by queer folks under the age of 25. The group's goal is to create a safe environment in which queer youth across the United States can feel joy and empowerment. In March 2023, Queer Youth Assemble organized a nationwide school walkout to protest recently passed anti-LGBTQ+ laws. Although most of the

The work of activist organizations has led to LGBTQ+ people being freer to share their identities openly.

ZOOM IN: FINDING REFUGE

Queer Americans aren't alone in being discriminated against because of their identities. In some parts of the Middle East, Africa, and Southeast Asia, it is dangerous and sometimes illegal to be queer. Queer families are often forced to leave their home countries to stay safe. Sweden, Argentina, and Kenya are a few countries that welcome LGBTQ+ refugees seeking asylum. In Europe, the United Nations Refugee Agency helps refugees complete the immigration process, find a place to live, and learn about LGBTQ+ protection laws. Queer refugees and their families are then able to build new lives in a safe environment.

participants weren't old enough to vote, they made their voices heard. They fought for the future they want to see for themselves and those who come after them. Platforms such as TikTok and Instagram have been used to amplify the actions and voices of the LGBTQ+ community, as well. They have become places for education, entertainment, and advocacy. Mercury Stardust is a TikToker. Known as the Trans Handy Ma'am, Stardust teaches viewers how to do simple home repairs. Her target audience is vulnerable renters who may not want a stranger coming into their homes. "You are worth the time it takes to learn something new," she says as she shows how to patch a hole in the wall or unclog a sink. Her passion for compassionate teaching led her to publish a how-to guide called *Safe and Sound: A Renter-Friendly Guide to Home Repair.*

In 2023, Stardust and fellow trans-woman and TikToker Jory fundraised more than $2 million for Point of Pride. This LGBTQ+ organization strives to empower low-income trans folks by distributing free gender affirming tools such as binders and shapewear to qualifying applicants. It also hosts the Annual Trans Surgery Fund to assist those who may not be able to afford the surgeries they need. Gender affirming surgeries can cost thousands of dollars. Point of Pride, along with many other groups that have similar surgery scholarships, is making gender affirming care more accessible to those who need it.

TikTok isn't the only place to find people leading change in the media. Queer folks continue to be better represented in movies, TV shows, and music. LGBTQ+ characters appear right alongside their straight counterparts in shows such as *Steven Universe*, *Modern Family*, and *Glee*. In a world where information is widely available and shared, people can watch their favorite celebrities discover their own gender identities and sexualities. When musician Demi Lovato changed her pronouns from "she/her" to "they/them" and back again, other nonbinary people took that journey with her. They learned that it's OK to change your mind. It doesn't make the journey any less valid.

When trans actor Elliot Page transitioned during the filming of the show *Umbrella Academy*, his character, Viktor, transitioned, too. This was a huge moment in TV history for the trans community. It set an example for future transitioning actors to not be afraid to be themselves.

As more nonbinary actors take the stage, organizations that give awards are faced with the issue of gendered categories. The Academy Awards and Tony Awards, for example, still use "Best Actor" and "Best Actress," rather than "Best Performance." Some nonbinary actors such as Justin David Sullivan and Asia Kate Dillion have expressed that they would rather not be nominated at all than be forced into a category that doesn't fit who they are. Some awards shows, such as the Spirit Awards, have made the change to gender neutral categories, showing that change is possible.

While the United States has made great strides in its treatment of the LGBTQ+ community since colonial days, the fight for equality continues. A person doesn't have to be famous to make a difference. Little changes, such as supporting a friend or family member, speaking up against bullying, and living a life that is true to oneself, can positively impact the community. Just as queer mavericks of LGBTQ+ history paved the road to today, the changes made now will provide a beacon of hope for generations to come.

ZOOM IN: QUEER JOY

When it comes to happiness, it's usually the simple things that bring people the most joy. Members of an LGBTQ+ community in southern Minnesota were asked, "What brings you queer joy?" Here's what they said:

- Seeing my kids express their queerness without hesitation

- Seeing other visibly queer couples in public, especially if they are older adults

- Wearing cute dresses

- Hearing my family use my correct pronouns

- Reading LGBTQ+ books with happy endings

- Going to Pride

- Being able to live authentically with other friends and community members living their lives just as vibrantly

Getting Real

JAMES BALDWIN

American writer James Baldwin was born in Harlem in 1924. He was one of eight children, and his family lived in poverty for most of his childhood. When his father died, he helped his mom raise his siblings. His favorite place to escape was the library. It was there that he found his passion for writing.

As a teen, Baldwin was disturbed by the feelings he was having toward other men. He had a religious upbringing, so he turned to the church to rid him of his lustful thoughts. He began preaching when he was only 14 years old. Then, in 1941, he left home to earn more money for his family. It was during this time that he allowed himself to be true to his heart. He was a gay Black man—and proud of that fact.

Baldwin wrote for newspapers and journals until 1948, when he headed to Paris, France. His first book was *Go Tell It on the Mountain*. It was about living as a Black man in the United States. The theme was common in a lot of his writing.

Baldwin continued to travel and write about racism, being gay, and interracial relationships.

His writing was hard hitting and honest, and it covered many controversial topics. When Baldwin returned to America, he participated in the Civil Rights Movement alongside Martin Luther King, Jr.

Baldwin died of cancer in 1987. His 29 books, as well as his hundreds of essays, plays, and poems, continue to influence and inspire readers.

ZOOEY ZEPHYR

Zooey Zephyr is a bisexual and transgender representative in Montana. Born in Billings, in 1988, Zephyr later studied at the University of Washington before getting a job at the University of Montana.

Zephyr became involved in activism in 2020. She wanted to ensure that the laws being passed wouldn't harm the LGBTQ+ community. De-

spite her efforts, she felt her voice was not being heard. So, she decided to run for representative in 2022. Zephyr won the midterm election and became the first trans lawmaker in Montana.

In 2023, Zephyr made headlines when she stood up against anti-trans laws in Montana. She confronted her colleagues and explained that denying health care to trans youth would increase suicide rates. She said the lawmakers would be at fault for their deaths and "have blood on [their] hands." For "breaking decorum," and because of her unapologetic defiance, she was banned from speaking on the House of Representatives chamber floor for the rest of the 2023 session. Her supporters were angry. They loudly chanted, "Let her speak!" before they were all removed from the House.

Despite being unable to speak on the chamber floor, Zephyr continued to advocate for the trans community from outside the House of Representatives. She was named to the 2023 TIME100 Next list. It recognizes rising leaders in politics, business, sports, entertainment, and more who are shaping the world. Zephyr will seek reelection in 2025.

Timeline

1600s
Puritans set up colonies in eastern North America and establish sodomy laws.

1950
The first long-lasting gay organization is formed— the Mattachine Society.

1962
Illinois becomes the first state to disband sodomy laws.

1965
The first Annual Reminders picket happens.

1969
The Stonewall Riots spark a queer revolution.

1970
The first Pride parade takes place, called the "Gay Liberation March."

1970
Marsha P. Johnson and Sylvia Rivera help found Street Transvestites Action Revolutionaries (STAR) to help unhoused trans youth.

1977
Harvey Milk is elected as the first openly gay man in public office in California.

1978
Gilbert Baker designs the first Pride flag.

1980
The AIDS epidemic begins.

1987
ACT UP is founded to bring attention to AIDS-related issues.

1999
President Bill Clinton establishes June as Lesbian and Gay Pride Month.

2003
The U.S. Supreme Court overturns sodomy laws and decriminalizes LGBTQ+ relationships.

2004
Same-sex marriage is legalized in the United States for the first time, in Massachusetts.

2011
President Barack Obama expands Pride month to include all LGBTQ+ people.

2013
The U.S. Supreme Court overturns the Defense of Marriage Act (DOMA).

2015
Same-sex marriages are fully legalized in the United States.

2023
A record number of anti-trans bills are proposed and passed in various U.S. states.

Glossary

advocate—to publicly support or fight for a person, group, or cause

cisgender—having a gender identity that matches one's gender assigned at birth

colony—a territory under the control of another country and occupied by settlers from that country

deadname—to call someone by a name they no longer associate with

detransition—taking actions to go back to one's gender assigned at birth

discrimination—applying different treatment to someone based on factors other than individual merit, such as race, gender, or income

gender affirming care—social, psychological, behavioral, and medical interventions that are designed to support and affirm a person's gender identity when it conflicts with the gender they were assigned at birth

gender dysphoria—significant distress caused when one's gender identity conflicts with their gender assigned at birth

gender identity—the personal sense of one's own gender

homophobia—the fear or hatred of people who are in the gay or lesbian community

misgender—to refer to someone by pronouns or gendered terms that don't align with their gender identity

mutual aid—the voluntary exchange of resources and services for the benefit of a community

sexual orientation—a person's identity in relation to the genders they are attracted to

transition—to take physical, social, or legal actions toward aligning with one's gender identity

Selected Bibliography

American Library Association. "Censorship by the Numbers." April 20, 2023. http://www.ala.org/advocacy/bbooks/by-the-numbers.

Bronski, Michael. *A Queer History of the United States.* Boston, Mass.: Beacon Press, 2011.

Centers for Disease Control and Prevention. "HIV Basics." December 1, 2022. https://www.cdc.gov/hiv/basics/index.html.

Duberman, Martin. *Stonewall: The Definitive Story of the LGBTQ Rights Uprising That Changed America.* New York: Plume, 2019.

Kayal, Philip M. *Bearing Witness: Gay Men's Health Crisis and the Politics of AIDS.* Boulder, Colo.: Westview Press, 1993.

PBS. "James Baldwin Biography." November 29, 2006. https://www.pbs.org/wnet/americanmasters/james-baldwin-about-the-author/59/.

Rouse, Wendy L. *Public Faces, Secret Lives: A Queer History of the Women's Suffrage Movement.* New York: New York University Press, 2022.

Websites

Gay, Lesbian, and Straight Education Network
https://www.glsen.org/resources/student-and-gsa-resources

Learn ways to make your school more LGBTQ+-inclusive.

The Trevor Project
www.thetrevorproject.org

Explore the nonprofit organization's educational materials and support tools for LGBTQ+ youth.

youth.gov
https://youth.gov/youth-topics/lgbt

Discover facts about living as LGBTQ+ youth in the United States.

Index

14th Amendment, 26, 27

Acquired Immune Deficiency Syndrome (AIDS), 14, 15, 16, 19, 26, 46

Annual Reminders, 16, 46

asexual, 23, 24, 30

Baldwin, James, 44

bisexual, 8, 23, 45

book banning, 29, 30

Cashier, Albert, 12

Catt, Carrie Chapman, 12, 15

cisgender, 8

Colonial America, 11, 46

Defense of Marriage Act (DOMA), 26, 27, 46

definition, acronym, 13

DeLarverie, Storme, 23

Fauci, Dr. Anthony, 15

Florida, 33

entertainment industry, 41

gay, 8, 14, 17, 19, 23, 38, 44, 46

gender, 8, 12, 24, 33, 42

gender affirming care, 33, 34, 37, 41

gender identity, 33, 34, 37, 42

gender dysphoria, 37

Gender Queer, 30

Hay, Mary Garrett, 12, 15

Human Rights Campaign, 38

intersex, 23

Kramer, Larry, 19

Lavender Scare, 17

laws, 11, 16, 26, 29, 34, 38, 40, 43, 46

lesbian, 8, 15, 23

Lesbian and Gay Pride Month, 23, 46

LGBTQ+ community, 8, 16, 17, 19, 20, 23, 24, 26, 29, 30, 33, 34, 38, 41, 42, 45

marriage, same-sex, 26, 27, 33, 46

National American Woman Suffrage Association (NAWSA), 15

Oberfell v. Hodges, 27

plus sign, 23

Point of Pride, 41

population, 8, 34

Pride parades, 20, 23, 41, 46

queer joy, 42

Queer Youth Assemble, 38

questioning, 23

Reagan, Ronald, 16

refugees, 40, 41

Roswall, Craig, 16

safe states, 34

same-sex couples, 16, 20, 26, 27, 29, 42

schools, 29, 33, 37

Stardust, Mercury, 41

Stonewall Riots, 16, 17, 23, 24, 46

symbols
    Ace rings, 24
    Blåhaj the Shark, 25

flags, 20, 24, 25, 46

lavender, 24

TikTok, 26, 41

trans community, 26, 34, 42, 45

transgender, 8, 11, 12, 23, 26, 33, 34, 45

transitioning, 34, 37, 42

trans refuge states, 34

two spirit, 23

U.S. Supreme Court, 26, 27, 33, 46

Wilde, Oscar, 24

Women's Rights Movement, 15

youth, queer, 8, 37, 38

youth, trans, 29, 37, 45, 46

Zephyr, Zooey, 45